INVISIBLE PEOPLE FOR HIRE

LOUIS PICKETT

www.dmchadwick.com

First published in 2020 by D.M. Chadwick
South Australia, Australia

Copyright © D.M. Chadwick 2019

ISBN 978-0-6485209-5-5

Author's Preface

Sam Hennessey, my editor, has suggested that I write a preface to my book. As I compose this preface, I have not yet completed what will be my debut novel, Invisible People for Hire. A labour of love 18 months in the making.

I would like to start by emphasising that I am a previously unpublished author. I approach this task with much trepidation. I do not have formal training as an author. The only subject at university I have completed related to writing was 'Editing for Publication'. It was a course that I found mildly insightful but in the end unsatisfying. My training comes from research, and that research is reading. I read books every day. Books that are on the New York Times bestsellers list and books I find covered in a thin layer of dust at the local library. I have read books without ceasing for as long as I can remember. My interest in writing began when I was in primary school. I would often write short stories and the occasional poem as a way to express feelings and emotions.

That is all to say it was not my education or writing experience that made me attractive to a publisher. I am still mystified that a publisher would request and pay an advance (small as it may be) for a work from a completely unknown author. Maybe that's just the state of the creative market at the moment?

This novel is about people trying to achieve things. The characters have objectives which they are struggling to achieve. I think it is true that there is something we all want to achieve in life. I hope that message comes across in this novel. I hope it will be a piece which readers will finish with a sense of immense satisfaction. I would much rather have a book which is satisfying to read, rather than a Harry Potter which sells millions of copies. The publisher may feel differently, but I will leave it up to Sam Hennessey to decide how to attract readers to this book.

I don't know if it's somewhat needy to ask, but if you read and enjoyed this novel, please leave a good review wherever you purchased this novel. That is only if you think this novel deserves praise. If it doesn't match your expectations, leave a negative review and I will think carefully about what you have to say. [Editor's Note: Please don't leave a negative review.]

By the time you are reading Invisible People for Hire, this book will likely have gone under many, many more revisions in pursuit of literary excellence. Anything less is not okay with me.

I do hope you enjoy this piece of literature.

Louis Pickett
April 2020

Editor's Preface

What makes a good book, good? About a year ago, I wondered if I no longer knew the answer to that question as I waded through dozens and dozens of mediocre manuscripts. I felt more tired with every folio I put in the growing rejection pile. I couldn't see any of them being a diamond in the coal mine of the saturated entertainment market.

Dozens of streaming services release a pile of new content each week. Thousands of books are released every month. Anyone can self-publish videos through YouTube or books through Amazon. The only thing that is a definite seller these days is a name. That's why Michelle Obama (who isn't even a career author), can demand an astronomically large advance on a book and publishers are willing to pay for it. There is no way a micro publisher like D.M Chadwick could afford to bid against one of the big five publishers for the output from a guaranteed selling author.

The only solution I could see was to bet small on a no-name author: a non-guaranteed seller, if you will. Obviously a no-name author demands a much lower upfront investment. I think that Louis, the author of this book, will readily admit that he is a no-name and understands this publisher's risk.

Don't misunderstand me: my goal and hope is that this book will sell a lot of copies. I hope it will sell like no other book that has come before. In the authors' preface, Louis mentions Harry Potter. I want Invisible People for Hire's sales to double the entire series of Harry Potter. I want this novel to reach the level of sales of Don Quixote, A Tale of Two Cities and Lord of the Rings. Is this is realistic goal? Why not? Why not have the goal of having this novel be translated into every language available and sitting on every bookshelf that has ever been assembled anywhere in the world.

I chose Louis Pickett for this project for one reason and one reason alone. He's an unpublished author with no formal training and therefore has no baggage attached to his ideas. He has free reign on the story, the themes and ideas he wishes to tell. I will not be an editor of Louis in the traditional sense. The content will be released in its purist form, right or wrong. My role is to get the book to market and encourage its readership to grow.

Could Invisible People for Hire become a literary classic? I think only when it has been read by at least a thousand people can a community judge a book as being a 'classic', so I encourage you to buy Invisible People for Hire a thousand times and send it to a thousand people. Leave a review online and ask those thousand people to do the same.

Did you know that you, reader, by yourself, could excel Invisible People for Hire to the best seller lists? If you are wealthy, and so inclined, you could buy even just five thousand copies, and it would be considered a bestseller on most lists.

But I do get ahead of myself. First of all, just purchase two or three copies, and read the book for yourself. Then you can leave your review online and decide how many dozen more you would like to purchase each week for the next year or so.

I think the only way to judge if a good book is 'good' is to look at the sales figures. So thank you for purchasing this book and helping its momentum to being good.

Sam Hennessey
August 2020

Chapter One
An Interview with the CEO

The city was made up of a thousand buildings. Inside these buildings were thousands of offices—hives of activity visited by overworked bees. These coffee guzzling creatures were on a perpetual search for a buzz from their sweet, fortnightly lump of pay that would appear in their bank accounts.

On the southernmost block of the city, before the landscape turned into suburbs of houses, was a short office building under the shadows of skyscrapers. One of the building's owners, sometime many years ago, had decided to render it in a custard-cream exterior which overtime had grown closer to mustard-brown. The type of people who entered and exited this building wore suits that were a little duller than those businesspeople with offices in the skyscrapers. Their shoes had a few more marks, their phones were a few generations older, their bags were backpacks and faux-leather satchels.

The carpet-square adorned hallways inside this aging

building had been worn down by the footsteps of hundreds going quickly to their offices, quickly out of their offices to find an overpriced sandwich for lunch, quickly back into their offices to avoid meeting others in the halls, and quickly home again to enjoy a reprieve from the scent of mouldy cracked pipes in the ceilings.

One of these businesspeople, a thirty-one-year-old man with a freshly shaven chin, screwed up his nose as a whiff of the mould hit his nostrils. He moved briskly down the hallway, fumbling for the office key in the front pocket of his backpack. He arrived at his office and pushed the key towards the keyhole. It slipped and made another small scratch in the door's white paint, revealing a forest-green undercoat. He tried again with the key and succeeded. He took a quick glance at the sign on his door and wondered if it was big enough. Printed in black ink on a sheet of white, laminated A4 paper and fastened to the door with double sided tape, was his name and business:

ALAN FLORES
INVISIBLE PEOPLE FOR HIRE

He noticed one of the corners had come unstuck from the tape during the night. It re-adhered with a small push and looked like it would hold firm, at least until the next day.

The office inside was minimally furnished—just a laminated-wood desk, a black faux-leather desk chair (both had come with the office lease), a black visitor's chair which Alan had 'borrowed' from a communal meeting room down the hall and a small bookshelf containing six binder folders of six different colours. They were all empty, only for show. The only decoration on the white walls was a framed four-by-three-foot photograph. In the photograph was tiered metal seating, all apparently empty apart from Alan, who sat alone straight and proud in the middle of the first row, wearing a pastel-green shirt and emerald-green tie.

Alan, with the door closed behind him, proceeded to slowly get ready for his day at work. He removed his laptop, phone and two mandarins from his backpack. He placed his fruit and computer on the desk and stowed his backpack underneath, carefully lining up his morning tea mandarin and lunch mandarin towards the back of his desk. He removed a power adaptor from the top drawer of his desk and connected it between a power outlet on the back wall to his laptop. He lined up his mobile phone perpendicular to the desk, giving the volume rocker on the side of the phone a push to ensure it would ring loud and clear.

10 minutes after arriving, he felt ready. He logged into his computer and proceeded to check each of his business' online marketing channels.

His website had seen three hits during the night. It wasn't much, but it was more than the two from the night before. His social media accounts hadn't increased in followers from two. He looked at the ad platform expenses dashboard. He had spent four-dollar during the night. One person had clicked on an ad for the search term 'the invisible man', and another had found the ad in the search results 'party hire'. He checked his email, but neither searcher had contacted him through his website's 'contact me' form.

After a few more hours of tinkering online, he looked at the time and saw it was ten o'clock. He reached across his desk, picked up the morning-tea mandarin, and proceeded to peel it. The smell of sweet citrus burst into the air as he piled pieces of mandarin skin on his desk, to be taken to the bathroom bin down the hall when he had finished.

Alan was enjoying his first bite of the juicy fruit, when his phone began ringing loudly. Its powerful vibrations against the desk caused his mandarin-skin pile to topple over.

The number was private. His heart skipped a beat, not only at the loud noise that had broken the silence, but also at the prospect of a new client.

He answered the phone enthusiastically. "Invisible people for hire. This is Alan speaking."

The caller hesitated for a moment before speaking. "Is this invisible people for hire?"

"Yes, it is. Who am I speaking with?"

The woman seemed almost reluctant to give up her name. "Karlie."

"Good morning, Karlie," Alan said. "How can I help you this morning?"

"I have a birthday...I am just wondering...What do you... do?"

It was the most frequently asked question of Alan's business, and he had a well-rehearsed answer. "I'm glad you asked. Let's say you're having a birthday, wedding, a casual get together-we haven't done a funeral yet, but I'm sure something could be arranged-let's say you're holding any event, but you want to 'wow' your friends and leave them talking for years to

9

come. You could spend thousands of dollars on fancy cakes, mildly amusing clowns or mediocre magicians. You could hire an overpriced DJ to play overplayed pop music or, for a much more economic fee, you could hire an invisible person to attend your party."

"An invisible person?" Karlie repeated.

"That's right. You don't need to feed them, they'll leave exactly when you want them to leave, and don't require a tip at the end of the event."

"So, what, you send like a dated certificate saying 'an invisible person attend this party'..."

Alan frowned. This wasn't the first time someone had requested a certificate of proof. "Yes, I can send a certificate, but the real draw card, for most people, is just having the invisible person attend their party."

"Hang on. So, you're saying that a real invisible person will come-"

"-if they're at your party and you can see them, they're not working for me, because then they wouldn't be a real invisible person."

"But invisible people aren't real, obviously."

This was always the aspect of his business that seemed to really make potential clients hesitate. "How do you know that?"

"Well, I've never seen one!"

Alan smiled and sat back in his chair, allowing Karlie to come to her own conclusion. "You're going to say that's because they're invisible."

"Correct. It will be the talk among your friends for years to come. Other party businesses charge upwards of two-hundred dollars an hour for whatever they do. Given the uniqueness of our service, we think we offer a fantastic deal."

There was another pause on the line. "Okay, fine I'd like to go ahead and make a booking, please."

Alan opened the calendar on his computer and tried to not reveal too much excitement in his voice. "Excellent. You've made a wonderful decision that you won't regret. Now, when is your birthday party?"

"It's actually my son's birthday party. He's turning twelve in a few weeks and was the one that found your ad online."

Alan paused typing. "A twelve-year-old boy's birthday? I should just let you know that we don't normally do birthdays for people under eighteen."

"Why not?"

"It's just... invisible people aren't really appropriate for minors. They can be somewhat misleading in their self-representation."

"I don't follow."

Alan sighed deeply. "We've had an unfortunate incident in the past where an invisible person, I believe it was Richard, was booked to attend a young man's Bar Mitzvah. Even though Richard was there on time, this young man was most disgruntled with Richard's appearance, or lack thereof. To put it bluntly, the young man didn't believe that Richard was in attendance and put up such a fuss that the parents asked for their money back. Since then, it has been a rule that invisible people don't attend celebrations involving minors."

"Well of course the young man didn't believe there was a real invisible person in attendance. That should be no reason

11

for my son's birthday. I promise he knows that invisible people aren't real, and therefore we won't ask for our money back."

Alan frowned. "Invisible people aren't real?"

The lady exhaled a laugh. "I'm sorry. Of course they're real."

"They are real."

"Yes, absolutely."

"You don't sound like you believe me."

"No, I do believe you. I absolutely do."

"I can prove it to you."

The mirth in the lady's voice began to fade away. "No, I don't need it proved to me. I'm sorry, but I am in a hurry. Are you able to send an invisible person to my son's birthday? Do you take card over the phone."

"It's not about money, ma'am."

"What is your fee? A hundred?"

Alan's fee for having an invisible person attend a celebration wasn't anywhere close to a hundred. "I'm sure we could arrange two invisible people to attend for that fee."

"Well...okay. Can I please book two invisible people to attend his party next Saturday?"

"Next Saturday," Alan repeated as he looked over the calendar on his computer. "Next Saturday I have Imogen Fentworth and Richard Jones available. They are both excellent invisible people, and I promise you will not see but a shadow of them."

"Okay," the woman said slowly. "That sounds fine by me."

"Excellent. I'll book you in!"

Alan recorded the woman's address and hung up the phone feeling victorious. This was his biggest booking yet, and he

12

felt he needed to reward himself. He decided he would go to a nearby cafe for a coffee and piece of apricot slice.

Just as he was slipping his arm into his jacket, his friend, Edward, burst into the room. Edward worked in another office building just down the street from Alan.

"Good morning?!" Edward asked enthusiastically.

"Good morning to you too!" Alan replied with equal enthusiasm. "I just booked a one-hundred-dollar gig next Saturday."

Edward slumped down into the visitor chair. "One-hundred-dollars? How did you manage that?"

"That was the fee she offered. I've rostered Imogen and Richard to attend. I'm heading out for a coffee"

Edward ignored him. "Next Saturday? Didn't you say Richard asked for that off for his daughter's birthday?"

"Did I?" Alan huffed. "That's not convenient! I already told the client that Richard will be attending."

"Just send Brent or Olivia instead. The client won't know."

"I'm not going to send someone in Richard's place. That would be plainly unethical. I'll have to call the client back and explain the situation."

Edward sat up excitedly. "Before you do, I have some great news to tell you. Do you remember how you were saying a few weeks ago how you felt like no one ever acknowledged how revolutionary your business is?"

Alan nodded expectantly.

"I've got you a date."

"Hang on. What's the connection between this revolutionary company and a date?"

"You can start the date by telling this girl all about this

13

business and how revolutionary it is. If she agrees, then you might as well propose marriage to her."

"A date? I don't have time go on a date," Alan gestured to the sparse office around him. "This is an empire I am starting here. I don't think now is the best time to start investing in relationships."

Edward laughed. "The reason you don't want to go on a date is because you're worried a relationship will get in the way of this business?"

Alan hesitated for a moment, then nodded. "A business needs focus and dedication; time to grow and thrive. If I take my attention away from this business...it could dwindle away."

"Come on, be honest. You've always talked about wanting to meet a girl one day and settle down. Now, suddenly when it could really happen, you are worried about your business?"

Alan removed his coat again as he began to feel warm under his collar. "Going on a date is a big step, you know. It's putting yourself out there.

"It is a big step," Edward agreed. "When I first went on a date with Katherine, I freaked out as well. But this girl, Chelsea, is really lovely. I'm sure you'll see she has many lovely qualities that could compliment your own."

"I feel like I should know more about this girl before I agree to a big step like a first date; a blind date, as this should more accurately be described."

Edward smiled slyly as he watched Alan begin to contemplate the proposal.

"Chelsea is one of Katherine's friends from work. She works in human resources. I've only seen her across the room twice or so at annual work dinners, but she's very beautiful."

"Very beautiful? I don't know if I should date someone that's very beautiful."

Edward laughed again, enjoying watching his business partner squirm at the conversation.

"This is a new you! You're normally very confident."

"I am confident. I am."

Alan sat back at his desk and unlocked his laptop. "What's her full name?"

"Chelsea Robins."

Alan searched for the name on Facebook. In the list of Chelsea Robins was one profile from the same area.

Alan turned the computer to show Edward. "Is this her?"

"That's her." Edward nodded.

"She is quite attractive," Alan admitted.

"So you'll go on the date?"

"I haven't said that yet. I still don't know that this is a good time for me and the business. We just won our biggest client today, and I want to win more just like it! What if a prospective client calls during the date? I'd need to take the call, and then I'd be seen as rude. I don't want to be known as a rude person. If you can book me meetings with prospective clients, that would be good. Please don't try and book me relationship meetings."

Edward rolled his eyes. "Then this is a business meeting."

"What is?"

"Chelsea Robins. Going to dinner with her is a business meeting. Maybe she has an event coming that could use the services of an invisible person."

"That could be a good way of looking at it," Alan said, warming up to the idea. "She's not weird or anything?"

"No, not that I know of."

Alan mulled it over, but finally declared. "Alright, I'll do it."

Edward clapped his hands together in glee. "Brilliant. I'll send you her phone number and you can set a time."

Alan nodded, but his mind was still dwelling on reservations against the meeting. "Is she invisible or visible?"

Edward appeared to have to think hard. "Reasonably visible, if I remember correctly."

"Good, good. Then I look forward holding a business meeting with her."

"You don't just have to talk business. You can talk about yourself," Edward said.

"Only if I come up in conversation."

Chapter Two
Visibly Nervous

The Lime had been constructed inside an old canoe shed on the edge of the river. Two of the outer brick walls had been demolished and replaced with floor to ceiling windows that revealed views across the river to parklands beyond.

Alan stood outside the front door of the restaurant, pretending to be interested in a small herb garden while he waited for his date to arrive. He had chosen a simple blue collared shirt and pair of chinos for the occasion; an outfit not too formal that it could appear he was too eager to please. He watched a small green hatchback car turn off the main road into the restaurant's car park. In the driver's seat was a young woman, her identity obscured by a pair of sunglasses. Alan's heart skipped a beat in the hope that this was Chelsea Robins. He pretended to continue to pay attention to a rosemary bush while the woman parked her car. He pretended to investigate the sage while the woman sat in the car for a long minute. Alan glanced up at the car. The woman hadn't moved from her car. He pretended to admire the basil as he heard the click of a car door, as it opened. He pretended to smell a plant, for which he didn't have the faintest idea it's name or purpose, while the woman walked across the car park; herself pretending to have an admiration for the clouds in the sky.

Alan stood up straight as the woman approached. "Chelsea?"

The woman smiled and nodded. "Alan?"

Alan thrust his hand out. "That's right. Alan Flores, Invisible People for Hire."

Chelsea hesitated for a moment, but switched her handbag to her other arm and shook the offered hand. "Very nice to meet you, Alan."

Alan thanked himself in abundance for agreeing to go on the date. He liked her already.

Alan looked up at the restaurant's name, high up on the building. "Have you ever been to The Lime before?"

"No, I have not," Chelsea said. "I've driven past in countless times, but never had an occasion to come here."

"I have never been here either, but I looked up the menu online and the dishes look exquisite and very expensive."

Chelsea nodded. "I looked as well. It's a very impressive restaurant."

"But you don't need to worry. I'll pay."

"That's very kind."

"Shall we go inside?"

Alan opened the front door and allowed Chelsea through first. The decor inside followed the trends of modern

18

restaurants. The theme of the building was bare brick with wooden tables and chairs and earthenware crockery. The quiet murmurs of diners already engrossed in conversation was heard under peaceful piano music coming out of overhead speakers.

They were greeted by a man standing behind a concierge podium with the warmest of smiles. "Good afternoon, Sir and Madam!"

"Good afternoon," Alan replied more confidently than he felt. "We have a reservation for two, under Alan."

The concierge looked down at the open book on the podium, running down the scribbled names with the back of his pen. He found the entry with delight. "Ah, Alan! Here you are. Would you please follow me?"

The concierge led Alan and Chelsea between seated restaurant patrons to a table placed right against the floor-to-ceiling window that overlooked the river. The two sat down and waited as the concierge opened napkins over their laps and handed them menus.

"Would you like to see the wine menu?" the concierge asked.

Alan looked at Chelsea for her reaction.

Chelsea smiled at the concierge but shook her head. "Just water for me, thank you."

Alan shook his head, so the concierge left for the two to peruse their menus. In near silence, the two pretended to look intently through the menu options.

After reading the description of a filet mignon for the 15th time, Alan decided it was time to make conversation. "So, how has your day been today?"

"Fine, fine thank you," Chelsea replied. "I had the day off so I was able to get some jobs-"

"-what do you do for work?" Alan interrupted eagerly.

"I work in sales for Harry's Furniture in Smithfield."

"Furnitures sales? How did you end up in furniture?"

"It's not my long term career plan. I got the job through a friend, and haven't quite worked out what I want to do...long term."

"We all have to start somewhere," Alan said. Chelsea gave a thin lipped smile and looked back down at her menu, so Alan did the same.

"So Katherine said understand you run a... party planning business?" Chelsea finally broke the silence with.

"No. Is that how she described it?"

Chelsea shrugged shyly.

"The business that I run is called Invisible People for Hire. It's a service where people can hire invisible people to attend their events."

Chelsea struggled to hide her confusion. "Oh. That's-"

"-it's a fantastic company that has seen nothing but success so far."

"I'm very glad to hear of your success."

"Do you have an event coming up?"

"I-"

"-it can be anything. Birthday, wedding. I haven't done a funeral yet, but I can imagine having an invisible person in attendance could help fill in seats."

Chelsea shook her head. "I'm honestly a little confused

about these invisible people-"

"-are they really invisible or do I just say I've sent an invisible person?" Alan finished the question for her. "The people I employee are one hundred percent invisible."

"But are they...real?"

Alan frowned. "What is real? Are we real? Or are just combinations of atoms travelling through a vast void of nothingness?"

Chelsea had no response but to sip on her glass of water.

Alan's frown slowly morphed into a smile. "I'm kidding. I'm not that philosophical. I find people that are too philosophical incredibly annoying! Are you philosophical?"

Chelsea shrugged. "I'm not sure-"

"-and I think that's a good indication that you're not. People that are too philosophical like to brag just how philosophical they are."

Chelsea tapped on her glass, wondering if she could make an excuse to end the date.

Alan noticed her unenjoyment. "I'm sorry. I keep talking. You can talk now."

"I haven't been on a blind date before."

"I think we should start again."

"I think that could be a good idea."

The concierge approached their table. "Have you made your choices-"

Alan cut him off. "-thank you, but we're going to start this date again. Could you please go back to the concierge desk and re-set this table? We'll enter again from outside."

Chelsea and the concierge both looked at Alan with the

appropriate amount of confusion.

"I meant just the conversation," Chelsea said. "We don't have to go outside and come in again."

"Oh." Alan gave an awkward chuckle. "I guess that would save time."

"So... can I suggest the lamb?" the concierge asked.

Alan quickly re-perused the menu. "Yes, the lamb for me, thanks."

"I'll have the chicken," Chelsea said.

The concierge left briskly with the menus.

"So, starting again." Alan inhaled deeply through his nose. "Hello, my name is Alan."

Chelsea smiled. "My name is Chelsea. It is nice to meet you, Alan."

"Likewise. What do you do for a living, Chelsea?"

"I am a saleswoman for a furniture store."

Alan raised his eyebrows in faux-surprise. "A furniture store? That's intriguing. And what do you like to do in your spare time."

"I have a few hobbies. I like to paint."

"You like to paint? That's interesting. What do you paint?"

"Lately I've been doing watercolour landscapes. What about you? Do you dabble in any arts in your spare time?"

"I've never been much of an artist, except in business. I think business could be defined as an art, per se."

"And your invisible people business-"

"-you haven't asked what my business is yet."

Chelsea played along. "What business do you run?"

"I run a party hire business where people can hire invisible people to attend events, parties et cetera."

"And these invisible people. Can you see them?"

"No, they are one hundred percent invisible."

"I mean, can you see them?"

"No, I don't have magical powers or anything."

"Can you hear them?"

"No."

"Can you... smell them?"

"Don't know. Never tried."

"Then how do you know that these invisible people are real?"

"They're real alright. Real enough that I had to fire one yesterday, which is a big deal, as you can imagine, as invisible people are not easy to come by."

"Why did you fire one?"

Alan took a drink and settled back in his chair. "I had this employee. His name was Graeme Smith. I had rostered him to attend a 21st birthday last Saturday. At about 7pm on the Saturday, I received a call from the party organiser that they hadn't seen any invisible people arrive. After reassuring her that Graeme was probably there in attendance but doing his job—being invisible—I texted Graeme, and it turned out that he had completely forgotten about the party. That meant, of course, that I had to call up the party organiser and profusely apologise and give them a refund. I couldn't allow that to happen again. I pride my business on being completely transparent."

Chelsea smiled. "Transparent. I get it."

Alan wasn't sure what she meant. "I can only imagine that

life as an invisible person is incredibly difficult. Think about the invisible children, for instance. One minute, they're there in front of you, the next minute, they're not there. Or they could be. You'd never know."

Chelsea struggled to hide her scepticism any longer. "This invisible person thing seems very far-fetched."

"It does take a while to fully understand."

The concierge returned to the table with their meals and placed them in front of the diners. Alan's meal was two small lamb chop on a bed of potato mash, surrounded by small pieces of orange, purple and white carrots.

After the concierge was out of earshot, Alan whispered. "It looks like some of this food is invisible."

"I think it looks delicious," Chelsea said.

They ate in silence. Alan was happy this business meeting was going so well.

"I've really enjoyed getting to know you," Alan said.

To Chelsea, this blind date had been anything but a success. "It's been interesting to hear about your work."

"So, what would you like to do next time we catch up?"

"I'm not sure-"

"That's alright. We can decide later."

Half an hour later, they left The Lime with their coats on, as a cool breeze had crossed over the river.

They walked across the car park together without exchanging any words.

Chelsea pointed to her car. "Well, this is mine. All the best with your business. It was very nice to meet you."

"Likewise," Alan said. "I do think we should catch up again."

Chelsea smiled. "I wish you all the best with your business."

Alan said thank you and went to his car. He watched in the rear-view mirror as Chelsea drove away. He quickly pulled out his phone and called Edward.

"Edward! The date went great!" Alan said when his friend finally answered the call.

"That is great to hear," Edward replied. "Chelsea's a great girl, and I wish you all the best together."

"Although, I will admit, she was a bit quiet."

"Did you let her speak?"

"Of course I let her speak!" Alan said defensively. "There were many moments of silence."

"Are you sure it went well?"

"I thought it did-"

His phone vibrated in his hand, and he looked at the screen to see a text message from Chelsea: 'Hi Alan, thank you for dinner tonight. I once again wish you success with your business. I don't feel that we could go any further relationally. Have a good night, Chelsea :)'

"Are you there?" Edward asked.

"Yeah. I just received a text from Chelsea. Apparently dinner didn't go as well as I thought. She's not keen to catch up again."

"I'm sorry to hear that, bud!"

Alan sighed. He realised the message had come through so quickly since Chelsea drove from the restaurant that she must have pulled over just to send it.

"I promise, if I think of any other single girls, I'll try and hook you up," Edward said.

"It's okay."

"Oh, by the way, while I've got you, one of Katherine's other friend's sister is having her 21st birthday party, and we were thinking it could be cool to hire an invisible person. Do you know if one of your people is available next Friday night?"

"Yeah, I'm sure there's someone," Alan said. "Email me the details and I send Lyle or Cameron or Angela along."

The two men wished each other good night and Alan ended the call with a heavy heart. He drove home to his apartment in silence, watching with envy couples laughing and having a good time in cafes that he drove past.

As soon as he got home, he put on his pyjamas and sat in front of the television to watch whatever he could find with the least amount of effort. He didn't fall asleep for hours but played the dinner over and over again in his mind, which eventually sent him off into a slumber.

Chapter Three
The Party

On Monday morning, Alan found himself sitting at his desk, staring at the wall. He thought he had let Chelsea go, but his mind kept flashing back to first seeing her in the car park on Saturday night and all the opportunity that that had presented—opportunity squandered because of reasons he didn't quite understand. He took a swig of his mochaccino and opened his laptop to check how his ads were performing when he saw a text message from Edward arrive. It was the details of the party he had mentioned.

Alan looked at his availability roster and began typing a reply with the details of Angela Charp. Angela was an invisible lady who often attended female-centric events such as baby and bridal showers. He was about to send the message, and maybe go for a walk or waste time some other way, when he had an idea that gave him a euphoric shot of hope.

He immediately called Edward and waited impatiently

while the phone rang. Just when he was about to hang up to try again in a few minutes, Edward answered. "Hey Alan, I'm at work at the moment. Is it urgent, or can I call you back on my lunch break?"

"It's urgent. I'm calling on business. Katherine's sister's friend's party. Is it females only, or will there be males there as well?"

"Males and females. Why?"

"No reason. I was going to send Angela Charp, but I think she is best suited to female only events."

"Okay," Edward said dismissively. "Is there someone else available you can send."

"Well, there is Lyle... Hey, on a completely different subject, do you know when you're going to see Chelsea next?"

"Probably at this party."

Alan tapped his feet excitedly. He paused for a moment, pretending he was re-reading his availability roster.

"Oh, no! I've just realised Lyle is not available either! That's all my invisible people accounted for."

"You don't have any invisible people available?" Edward asked sceptically.

"It would appear I only have one!"

"Well then send them! I'm sure Katherine's friend won't mind what their name is."

Alan was sweating the following Saturday as he pulled up to the curb down the street from Katherine's friend's house. The street was packed with cars. It was a cold night, and yet to Alan it was swelteringly hot inside a green, bushy ghillie suit. He had hired one at a costume hire store, and although it took away all his profits from the night, he considered it a worthwhile investment. He squeezed himself out of his car and retrieved the matching head covering from his back seat. On his way back down the street to the house, he spotted a small green hatchback, Chelsea's car, and his heart leapt in his chest. He could hear loud, bassy music coming from the back of the house, so he walked down the driveway of the mid-century family home to find a party in full swing. A few dozen people of all ages, from teenagers to middle-aged folk were sitting or mingling in the vicinity of a grazing table covered in cheeses, cold-cut meats, fruits and desserts. A series of coolers were on the ground nearby filled with an assortment of beverages submerged in ice. Against the brick wall of the house were two large gold-foil helium balloons, a '2' and a '1'. Despite these attractions, when Alan passed through the gate into the backyard, all eyes turned to him. He stood there, still sweating profusely under the ghillie suit, beginning to second guess his idea. A silence had come over the party attendees, with only the pumping music and some mirthful chatter emanating from inside the house being the soundtrack to this strange arrival.

"I'm invisible!" Alan announced loudly.

Edward, who was standing next to some other men on the other side of the backyard began to laugh loudly, a laugh that rippled as a chain reaction to everyone present. Everyone assumed this new arrival was a friend of the birthday girl.

The birthday girl quickly approached Alan, adjusting her red party dress as she walked.

"Who is that under there?" she asked with a laugh, but

here eyes showed concern that someone had invited a weirdo.

"I'm an invisible person," Alan said. He hadn't thought of a great explanation for why he, as a supposed invisible person, could be seen. He was thankful that Edward quickly came over with a big grin. "Do you remember when I said I would get an invisible person to attend your birthday?"

"I thought you were just being silly. You actually found someone to..." she shook her head in defeat. "Well done, Ed. Very funny. Whoever you are in that costume, enjoy the party."

And with that she smiled and went away to continue mingling.

"You're the invisible person?" Edward asked as quietly as he could. "There was no one else available to send, so you decided to come yourself?"

"That's an adequate summary," Alan said.

Edward scoffed. "Well, have fun. There are a few bushes by the back fence you could blend in with."

Alan over exaggerated nodding his head so that it could be seen through the thick head piece. He made his way carefully through the party goers, being careful not to knock over a pair of young boys not looking where they were running. He arrived at the line of shrubs by the back fence, lit only by fairy lights hanging over head. Those that continued to watch him in the crowd laughed as he sat down on the paved garden edging, hunching his back to replicate a shrub.

He sat there, unmoving, for more than 15 minutes, watching the party evolve in front of him. He felt like a theatre patron, watching this intricate, loud play be performed for him alone. Groups of people stood together, talking over the tops of each other, endlessly smiling. There were occasionally

30

those that appeared lonesome, but they quickly connected into a nearby conversation or were joined by other lonesome attendees.

A makeshift dance floor of a rug that had been rolled out onto the grass went unused. Alan's eyes scanned across the party goers. A majority were young women in their early twenties who had evidently spent many hours preparing their immaculate facades of make up and varying hair styles. They chatted rapidly and without ceasing. The men also looked to be about the same age, and either tagged along into their female partner's conversations, or stood idly by with the other men throwing out morsels of conversation starters now and again to see if anything would start a decent dialogue.

There was, of course, the one particular party goer that Alan searched eagerly for among the crowd of faces. He was unable to see Chelsea from where he sat.

The two boys whom he had almost walked into earlier approached him and began hesitantly poking him in the shoulder, getting more and more relaxed at the lack of response, until one of the boys was about to poke him in the head. Alan suddenly stood up, sending the boys fearfully tripping backwards onto the grass with small yelps. The boys got up from the grass and ran away laughing to themselves.

Alan, feeling relief in his legs which had begun to grow stiff in the same position, decided to continue his search for Chelsea by going inside. He walked back through the crowds and made his way through the back door of the house into the living room. There were fewer people inside, many being older than the party goers outside, and they sat on chairs

31

around the perimeter of the room, talking quietly in respite of the loud music that blared outside.

Alan spotted her. Chelsea was sitting, turned away from the door, talking with another woman.

A number of those inside the house had not been witness to Alan's first entrance, and they audibly gasped at the appearance. Alan ignored the looks and sat up straight on a vacant chair near Chelsea. The girl to whom Chelsea was talking to stared quizzically at Alan, which caused Chelsea to turn around to see what was behind her. She exclaimed "Wow" in surprise and looked Alan up and down.

Alan didn't move. "Good evening.".

Chelsea reluctantly said "Hi" then turned back to her original conversation partner.

"I'm invisible," Alan said, unaware that Chelsea was no longer paying attention. After not hearing any response, he turned his head as best he could and said "Chelsea."

Chelsea swivelled in her chair to the person in the ghillie suit with great confusion. "Who is in there? Ben?"

"No, it's Alan. Alan Flores. From Invisible People for Hire."

"Oh, hello, Alan," she said with little warmth. "I didn't know that you would be here tonight."

"I was a late replacement. Edward hired an invisible person for the birthday, but everyone else was unavailable so I stepped in."

"I see."

Chelsea seemed to be at a loss for words, so Alan asked. "How have you been?"

"Good. Great, thanks- would you be able to take off the mask? It's a little weird talking to you when I can't see you."

32

Alan did as he was asked and removed the head piece. His hair was matted with sweat, and his face was a shade of deep red. He placed the head piece on his lap and gave Chelsea a smile.

"So you're here working tonight?" Chelsea asked.

Alan nodded. "Yes. This is my first party as an invisible person, believe it or not. How do you think I'm doing?"

Chelsea once again looked Alan up and down. "I'm not sure. You're the polar opposite of invisible in that outfit."

Alan shrugged. "I feared that, but it was the best invisible costume that I could come up with on short notice. Hey, I just wanted to discuss when we went out for dinner..."

He waited for Chelsea to interrupt with some sort of statement of regret about turning down a second date, but she stayed silent, so he continued.

"I just wanted to let you know that I really enjoyed myself, and I would like to catchup again."

Chelsea avoided eye contact and lowered her voice. "Thank you. It was a good... as I said in the text, I don't think our relationship would work. I'm sure there's a girl out there who would be much better suited for you, and I don't want to stand in the way of you finding that girl."

The words brought little comfort to Alan, but he smiled bravely. "I just wanted to double check."

Alan stood up. He turned to exit the lounge with his head piece under his arm when he knocked into someone. The man that had been holding the cup was a short man wearing a beige long-sleeve shirt, beige chinos and beige shoes. He blended in quite well with the beige painted walls of the lounge room. But now his beige outfit had a stream of bright orange soft drink dripping down his front.

"Oh, I do apologise," Alan said. "I didn't see you there!"

The man mumbled something quietly as he looked down at his outfit in disgust.

"What was that?" Alan asked.

The man repeated a little louder. "That's okay, don't worry about it."

Chelsea got up quickly from her chair and fetched some napkins from a nearby table. "Oh, Daniel! Are you okay?"

The man in beige just stood on the spot, looking down sadly at his clothes.

"I'm okay," he said quietly to Chelsea as she began mopping up the orange drink from the hardwood floor.

Everyone in the lounge room watched as Alan apologised again and again to Daniel. For ever apology, Daniel responded with a quiet 'It's okay'. Eventually, Alan could think of nothing more to say.

"Come to the laundry, Daniel," Chelsea said, beckoning the man away down the hall. "We'll see if we can find a sponge to clean your clothes."

Alan sighed, put on his head piece, and walked back outside. He gave a few fist pumps as he walked across the dance floor between a few party goers whose inhibitions had loosened, which was met with elation from onlookers.

He sat back down on the garden edge and again watched the party play before him. Party goers occasionally walked past him and laughed at the sight of a man trying to appear to be a bush. A group of them began to take selfies with him. He stayed completely still. After a few minutes, he saw through a lounge room window Chelsea and Daniel smiling and talking together as old friends.

He felt a pang of envy that would not go away.

After a half hour of watching the partiers becoming increasingly erratic, he pulled out his phone from a hidden pocket and saw that his billed hour was up. He rose from the garden edge and walked back through the crowds, a few who kindly patted him on his back. He left out the back gate and went to his car. He stripped off the head piece and ghillie suit, throwing it haphazardly onto the back seat. He had a t-shirt and shorts underneath, both drenched in sweat, but the cool night breeze brought immediate relief.

Without his disguise, he walked back down the driveway and through the back gate to the party. In stark contrast to his first arrival, no one looked at him. No one cared. It was another person arriving at the party. He walked through the crowds, all who had only minutes earlier being patting him on the back, to the drinks table and poured himself a beverage. He stood against a wall and nodded his head to the music. He looked up at the fairy lights, twinkling rapidly above, all dancing together in sequence. He didn't see who, but someone moved past him quickly, bumping his arm, causing a little of his drink to spill out.

"Sorry, mate. I didn't see you there!" the person called without stopping.

Alan nodded his head. "I see."

The End